Rhyme Time
Story Time

Written by Lorna Read
Illustrated by Jenny Tulip

Brimax · Newmarket · England

One to Ten and Back Again

One little puppy on his own
Looking for a juicy bone.

Two yellow ducklings on the lake.
What a quacking noise they make!

Three fluffy clouds say, "Goodbye, Sun.
We're floating off to find some fun."

Four silver fishes wave their tails.
Four red boats have four white sails.

Five furry kittens jumping high,
Trying to catch a butterfly.

Six little chicks with lots to do
Cross the farmyard two by two.

Seven swans swim on the stream.
How their clean white feathers gleam!

Eight little robins on a wall.
See if you can count them all.

Nine black horses run a race.
One has got a snow-white face.

Ten birthday candles brightly shine.
One goes out, now there are nine.

Nine brown cows stand by the gate.
One walks off and that leaves eight.

Eight pretty flowers in a row.
One is picked but seven still grow.

Seven little kittens getting up to tricks.
One falls asleep. Now there are six.

Six little frogs start to dive.
One's in the water. That leaves five.

Five black cats sit by the door.
One walks through and that leaves four.

Four red apples on a tree.
One falls off so that leaves three.

Three white doves say, "Coo, coo, coo."
One flies away and that leaves two.

Two puppies playing in the rain.
One goes home so there's one again.

Can you find the five differences between the two pictures?

Can you find all the animals in the picture?

one puppy

two kittens

three rabbits

four birds

Somewhere Warm to Sleep

Mr and Mrs Mouse live on the farm. They have eight baby mice who love to play and scamper about. The Mouse family live in the barn because the farmer stores his corn there. The mice love to eat corn!

Most mice are afraid of cats.
But the farm cat is so fat and
lazy that the farm mice play
all around her. She spends all
day asleep on a sack of corn
in the barn. Sometimes the baby
mice even swing from her tail!

"Brrrr!" says Mrs Mouse one morning when the Mouse family wake up. "This nest isn't warm enough for the cold weather. I think we will make a new nest. I need you all to help me. We will need some wool from the sheep, some hair from the horse, and some feathers from the hens."

The baby mice scamper off to the stable first. The farmer is brushing the horse. There is a lot of the horse's hair in the straw.

"Excuse me, Mr Horse, may we take some of this hair to use as a warm lining for our new nest?" asks one of the mice.

"Of course," says Mr Horse.
"I don't need it any more."

The baby mice then scamper to the sheep's field.

"Excuse me, Mrs Sheep, may we have some of your wool to make our new nest soft and warm?" ask the baby mice.

"Here you are," says Mrs Sheep. "I brushed some off this morning against the gate. It should keep you very snug."

The cows are sad that they have nothing to give the mice for their new nest. "We have no fur or wool to give you, but you may have some of this fresh milk to drink instead."

"Thank you," say the baby mice. "We love to drink fresh milk."

The mice scamper off to see the hens. They have just one more thing to collect - feathers.

The hens have dropped lots of feathers on the ground, and tell the mice that they can help themselves.

"Thank you," say the baby mice as they pick up all the feathers they can carry. Then they hurry back to the barn.

The new nest is in the corner of the barn. The baby mice show their mother and father the hair from the horse, the wool from the sheep and the feathers from the hens.

"Well done!" says Mrs Mouse. "We are going to have a very warm, snug nest now."

That night, as the moon shines down on the farm, all the animals are asleep. The cows and sheep are sleeping in the field. The horse is asleep in his stable. The hens are asleep in their coop. But the mice are the warmest of all in their soft, new nest.

Can you find the five differences between the two pictures?

Can you say these words and tell the story in your own words.

horse

sheep

cow

hen

Cock-a-Doodle-Doo!

Mother cow gives milk to drink.
The sound she makes is, "Moo."

A baby cow is called a calf.
It likes to drink milk, too!

This long-tailed animal is a horse.
He's very big and strong.

A baby horse is called a foal.
Its legs are very long.

Sheep give us wool to make our clothes.
They like green grass to eat.

A baby sheep is called a lamb.
Baa! Doesn't it look sweet?

This animal is a nanny goat.
She gives us cheese and milk.

A baby goat is called a kid.
Its coat is as soft as silk.

Hens lay fresh eggs for us to eat.
"Cheep!" say their baby chicks.

"Cock-a-doodle-doo!" the rooster cries,
Sitting on a heap of sticks.

A white duck swims upon a pond.
She's calling, "Quack, quack, quack!"

Her ducklings are too far away.
She wants them to come back.

The sheep-dog helps to herd the sheep.
She's running fast all day.

Her little puppies stay at home
And eat and drink and play.

The goose is such a noisy bird.
"Honk, honk," she says to all.

Her little goslings run around.
Oh dear, one has had a fall!

A daddy cow is called a bull.
His horns are very big.

"Please don't forget me," someone says.
Who is it? It's a pig!

Can you find the five differences between the two pictures?

Can you find all the animals in the picture?

horse

cow

sheep

pig

The Ducks' New Pond

It has been raining for days. The farmyard is very wet and muddy. The brown horse looks over his stable door. "Look, everyone, the rain has stopped at last!" he says. The cows and the sheep look up to see a big rainbow across the sky.

The rooster flies up to the roof
of the barn. He can see the
whole farm and across the field
from there. "Cock-a-doodle-doo!
The sun is coming out," he sings.
"And all the rain has made us
a new pond."

The ducks at the old pond are very excited. They hear what the rooster says.

"A new pond!" says Mrs Duck. "My ducklings would like some nice, fresh water to swim in. Come here, children. We are going to find the new pond."

The ducks waddle up the hill.
Mrs Duck is first and the smallest
duckling is last. They come to
a gate. All the ducklings walk
under the gate, but Mrs Duck
gets stuck. She wiggles and flaps.
Then with a big "Quack!" she
squeezes through.

The ducklings then reach the track where the farmer drives his tractor every day.

"We must make sure that nothing is coming," says Mrs Duck to her ducklings. They look left and then they look right. The farmer is coming with his tractor. He stops to let them cross the track.

The cows are going to the barn to be milked. The ducklings are crossing the farmyard at the same time.

The ducklings are very tiny and the cows have very big feet. "Excuse me, cows," says Mrs Duck. "Please stand still so that you don't step on my babies."

The new pond is across the field.
Mrs Duck counts her ducklings
to make sure they are all there.
One, two, three, four, five…one
duckling is missing.
"Where is he?" cries Mrs Duck.
The sheep-dog has rounded
up the little duckling with the
sheep.
"Come here," says his mother.

The smallest duckling is very tired. "I cannot walk any farther," he says. "I think I will stop and have a rest."

"We are nearly there now," says Mrs Duck. "Only a few more steps."

The smallest duckling's brothers and sisters help him for the last part of the journey.

The sun is shining brightly when they reach the pond.
The water looks cool and fresh.
"I am going to be first in the water!" quacks the smallest duckling excitedly.
"You soon forgot how tired you were!" laughs Mrs Duck as she and the rest of her ducklings join him in the new pond.

Can you find the five differences between the two pictures?

Can you say these words and tell the story in your own words.

rainbow

rooster

duckling

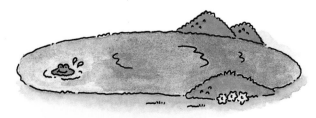

pond